Boxing Bootsie

by Shelley Swanson Sateren
illustrated by Deborah Melmon

CONTENTS

ADVENTURES at TABBY TOWERS

IT'S TIME FOR YOUR ADVENTURE AT TABBY TOWERS!

At Tabby Towers, we give cats the royal treatment. We are a first-class cats-only hotel that promises a safe, fun stay for all guests.

Tabby Towers has many cat toys and games. We make personal play time for every guest. And we have a large indoor kitty playground that will satisfy every cat instinct, including climbing and hunting. Also, your kitty will never tire of watching our cow and chickens from the big playground window.

We are always just a short walk away from the cats. Tabby Towers is located in a large, sunny, heated room at the back of our farmhouse. Every cat has a private litter box and a private, three-level "apartment", complete with bed, toys and dishes. Of course, we will follow your feeding schedule too.

TABBY TOWERS WHO'S WHO

KIT FELINUS

Kit Felinus (fee-LEE-nus) is a lifelong cat lover. She has worked for cat rescue and shelter operations much of her adult life. After seeing the great success of Hound Hotel – the dog hotel next door – she realized the need for a cat hotel in the area. So she started Tabby Towers. She now cares for cats all day long and couldn't be happier!

TOM FELINUS

Tom Felinus is certain that his wife, Kit, fell in love with him because of his last name, which means "cat-like". He is a retired builder. He built Tabby Towers' kitty apartments, cat trees and scratching posts. He built the playground equipment too, which will keep your kitty happy for hours.

TABITHA CATARINA FELINUS (TABBY CAT, FOR SHORT)

Tabby Cat is Kit and Tom's granddaughter and a true cat lover. In fact, the cat hotel is named after her! She helps at Tabby Towers in summer. The 8-year-old daughter of two vets, Tabby lives in the city and has her own cat. She's read almost as many books about cats as her grandma has! Tabby will give your kitty all the extra attention or playtime he or she may need.

Next time your family goes on holiday, bring your cat to Tabby Towers.

Your kitty is sure to have a purr-fect time!

CHAPTER 1
Furry FaceTime

I'm Tabitha Catarina – Tabby Cat, for short. Here's the truth about me: My personal world does *not* spin around the sun. My world spins around *cats*.

That's correct. I L-O-V-E, love them. Hairballs and all.

I've loved cats my whole life. Now I get to work with them every day at Tabby Towers. I'm *such* a lucky girl!

But there's a problem. A big one. And her name is Alfreeda Wolfe.

I'm talking about the girl next door. She lives on a farm next to my grandparents' place. Alfreeda L-O-V-E-S, loves dogs. That's okay, but she thinks dogs are the *best*. I, on the other hand, am an animal lover. Although I love cats most, I think *all* animals are great. I would never say anything mean about a dog.

Alfreeda really drove me crazy a few weeks ago. It was the day my very own cat, Bootsie, travelled from the city to the country to join me at Tabby Towers.

As usual, Alfreeda bragged about dogs and put down cats. She even said unkind things about my sweet, beautiful Bootsie!

I'm sure you're wondering if my "claws" came out. Well, get cozy, and I'll tell you all about it.

It was early in the morning, towards the end of June. I sprang out of bed like a cat. I pulled off my pyjamas and pulled on my leopard-print leggings and a Tabby Towers T-shirt.

I grabbed my silver locket. I opened it and kissed the tiny photo inside. It was a picture of my very best friend in the whole world – my cat, Bootsie.

I missed her *so* much. I'd been at my grandparents' farm for two weeks. Two whole weeks without Bootsie! I'd *never* been away from her for that long. I didn't know how much longer I could stand it.

I snapped the locket shut and kissed it again. I hung the chain around my neck and hurried to the bathroom.

First I cleaned my cat-eye glasses. I brushed my hair and pulled it into a high ponytail. I like it sticking up high, like the tail of a happy cat.

Then I brushed my teeth for two whole minutes, because I, like a cat, like to be fresh and clean at all times. I smiled at the mirror, then looked at the kitty-cat clock on the bathroom wall. *Good,* I thought. *I've got ten minutes before FaceTime with Bootsie.*

Ten minutes was just enough time for something I needed to do. I leaped up the attic stairs and dug through boxes on the attic floor. Soon I found some old picture frames. I grabbed a small one. It didn't have a photo inside. Purr-fect.

I ran back to my room and put my favourite photo of Bootsie into the frame. Her big blue eyes peered back at me.

"You're *so* sweet and *so* beautiful," I said out loud. "I miss you terribly, Bootsie! I wish I could talk Grandma Kit into letting you stay at the farm with me."

I put the frame on my bedside table and grabbed my mobile phone. Actually, the phone wasn't mine. It belonged to my parents. I was allowed to call only them or my nanny, Pam.

I called Pam more often than my parents. She was cat-sitting Bootsie for the summer at our apartment in the city. My parents were on location at a film set. They're both vets. They care for animals that appear in films. That's their job.

Using the phone's video app, I called Pam. "Hi, Pam," I said. "Where's Bootsie?"

"Good morning, Tabby Cat," Pam said with a yawn. She sat up in bed and rubbed her eyes. "Is it seven o'clock already? Do our daily calls *have* to be so early?"

"Yes!" I replied. "There's so much to do in the hotel. Once I get going, I'm busy all day."

"I believe it," Pam said. Then she called, "Here, Bootsie. Come and say hi to Tabby."

Seconds later, Bootsie appeared on my phone. My heart leaped.

Bootsie looked as beautiful as ever. Long, brown, fluffy hair covered her body. The fur on her face, ears, tail and feet was black. That's why I'd called her Bootsie. It looked like she wore black boots.

"Good morning, Bootsie!" I said.

She blinked and started to cry.

Oh no, I thought. *Not again.*

Pam quickly pulled Bootsie away from the phone. But Bootsie kept meowing. She sounded *so* sad.

Pam looked at me and shook her head. "Maybe we shouldn't do FaceTime every morning, Tabby," she suggested gently. "Bootsie cries only when she sees you or when she hears your voice. Honestly, she's been much better this week."

A lump grew in my throat. I couldn't reply.

"She really seems less lonesome without you now," Pam said softly. "I'm taking the very best care of her. I'm brushing her every day, giving her a lot of treats, playing with her often –"

"But I can't stand it anymore!" I cried. "I miss her too much!"

"We all agreed this is the best plan," Pam said in her firm nanny voice. "Bootsie will spend the summer in her own home. She wouldn't be happy at the farm, sharing space with all those other cats."

"How do we know that for sure?" I argued. "We could try! You could bring her here! I'm going to ask Grandma Kit again."

"All right." Pam sighed. "Just don't be too sad if the answer is no."

"Okay."

I said goodbye, turned off the phone and thought hard. I knew what Grandma Kit was going to say. But this time, I'd be prepared – with facts to prove my point!

CHAPTER 2

Keep up the stare-down

Ten minutes later, I was sitting on my floor in a sea of non-fiction cat books.

The books belonged to me. I'd brought them from the city. Of course, I'd read them all already – many times.

Now I searched for important parts to read again. Parts about cats guarding their territory. Cats believe certain areas belong to them. They will do almost anything to keep those areas safe from other cats or to make those areas larger. Sometimes they'll even fight.

The truth is, cats are more territorial than dogs. Of course, I'd *never* tell Alfreeda that. She'd brag about how some dogs are really laid-back. Well! I'd point out that Himalayan cats, like Bootsie, are known as one of the most "laid-back" types of cats.

But right then, I had to talk with Grandma Kit, not Alfreeda. For about twenty minutes, I read about how to keep indoor cats from acting too territorial. Then I hurried to find Grandma Kit.

I tiptoed past my grandparents' room. Grandpa Tom was still asleep. He's nocturnal, like all the guests at Tabby Towers. He knows that cats hunt at night. It's their instinct. So he always stays up late with our hotel guests. He plays predator-prey games with them. He makes them feel like they're hunting in the wild.

I hurried down the stairs, through the living room and into the kitchen.

I looked around for Scruffy. He's Grandma Kit's indoor-outdoor cat. He wasn't in his bed by the oven. I thought maybe he hadn't come indoors yet that morning.

It's not fair, I thought. *Scruffy gets this huge house all to himself. He doesn't even use most of the space!*

Scruffy always spent daytime hours sleeping. At night, he hunted mice in the barn and fields. He would never share the house with my Bootsie. He was much too territorial. Grandma Kit had said so.

I sighed and knocked on the door beside the refrigerator. It led to Tabby Towers, at the back of the house. My grandparents had turned their large family room into the cat hotel.

"Tabitha?" Grandma Kit called through the closed door. "Is that you?"

"Yes!"

"All clear!" she called.

"All clear" meant no cats or kittens prowled near the door, ready to spring past my feet. I opened the door carefully then shut it quickly behind me.

Two cute kittens – Fifi and her brother, Furbaby – played on a little see-saw. Grandpa Tom had made the see-saw. It sat at the centre of a large indoor kitty playground. Grandpa Tom had built everything in the fun play space.

A third guest, a beautiful Persian cat called Child, sat high on a cat tree. He peered out of the picture window at the chickens in the farmyard.

Child had long, fluffy hair just like Bootsie. Even a quick glance at him made my heart hurt all over again.

Grandma Kit stood at the sink, cleaning the cat-food dishes. "Good morning, Tabitha!" she said and grinned.

I patted Fifi and Furbaby on their cute, soft heads. Then I hugged Grandma Kit. Straight away, I got busy begging.

"I just saw Bootsie on my phone," I said. "She cried again."

"Don't worry," Grandma Kit said kindly. "She'll get used to being away from you. Just give her time."

"But I miss her!" I cried. "I *want* her here! I know she can't share the house with Scruffy. And she can't stay in my bedroom all summer. She wakes me up too much at night. But could Bootsie have one of the kitty apartments in the hotel? There's always at least one free."

Grandpa Tom had built seven kitty apartments. They were small, three-level units with screen doors and walls in-between. Each cat had its own safe, cozy, private space.

"Of course I'd be happy to let Bootsie have an apartment," Grandma Kit replied. "I don't like to board more than five guests at a time anyway. But *Bootsie* wouldn't be happy. She'd be too nervous here. She wouldn't like living with other cats for weeks on end. You know how you're an only child? How you need your quiet time because you're used to it?"

I nodded.

"Well, it's no different with Bootsie. She's always been your only pet. She's known the inside of your apartment – and nothing else – her whole life. She hasn't had to share anything with other cats. Bootsie *will* act territorial here. She's a *cat*. That's her instinct."

"I know, Grandma," I said. "I was just reading about that fact! Bootsie *wouldn't* act territorial here at Tabby Towers, though. Cats fight other cats when there isn't enough food or water.

They fight when there aren't enough warm beds or fun toys or litter boxes. Tabby Towers has more than enough of those."

Grandma Kit smiled. "Ah-ha. You're learning to think like a cat, Tabby Cat," she said. "But there are lots of reasons why cats sometimes act very territorial."

"Could we just try?" I begged. "*Please?*"

Grandma Kit's smile faded. "Cats really are happiest *and* healthiest in their own territory, in their own home," she said. "Pam is taking excellent care of Bootsie too."

"*Please,* Grandma!" I begged.

She stared at me. I stared at her. She didn't look away. Neither did I.

We both knew what a stare-down meant in the cat world. It meant a standoff – a silent battle between two territorial cats.

I kept staring. So did Grandma Kit.

My eyes stung and filled with tears. So did Grandma Kit's.

I forced my eyelids open even wider. I refused to look away or even blink.

Unfortunately, Grandma Kit refused too. We'd both met our match!

CHAPTER 3
Big crybaby cat

Seconds passed. My eyes remained open. I simply *refused* to blink!

Grandma Kit refused too.

Then, suddenly, she turned her head away. She blinked and rubbed her eyes!

In a true cat-to-cat stare-down, the first cat that looks away is the loser.

"I won!" I cried. "Oh, thank you, Grandma!"

She laughed and gave me a hug. "You're welcome, Tabitha," she said. "But listen.

Bootsie may really dislike Tabby Towers. If she can't get along with the other cats here, Pam *must* take her back to the city. Bootsie could become too nervous here. It wouldn't be healthy for her. Do you understand?"

I nodded. The thought of Bootsie having to leave Tabby Towers made me *so* sad. *That won't happen,* I thought.

"So which apartment should I put her in?" I asked excitedly.

"The one in the furthest corner," Grandma Kit said. She pointed across the room. "Bootsie will feel more hidden there. I'm sure she'll need a lot of alone time."

"Well, *I'm* sure she'll get along great with the other guests," I said. "She'll make friends."

"We'll see." Grandma Kit got busy washing the cat-food dishes again.

I dashed back to my room and grabbed my phone. I called Pam and told her the news.

"That's wonderful!" Pam said. "I'll start packing Bootsie's things. We'll be there in a couple of hours."

"I can't wait!" I said. "Can I say hi to Bootsie again right now?"

"I don't think that's a good idea, Tabby," Pam said. "I finally calmed her down from your other call. Oh no! She heard your voice! She's jumping straight at me!"

A furry rocket hit Pam's shoulder. Pam fell sideways and dropped the phone. It landed on the floor. Two seconds later, Bootsie stood over it. She leaned in. Her cute nose almost touched the phone. I could see her whole beautiful face.

She must've seen me, because she started to cry. *Meow! Meow! Meow*!

Pam grabbed the phone. "Okay, that's enough for now," she said. "Bye, Tabby! We'll see you soon!" She turned off her phone, and Bootsie disappeared.

"Do you get a lot of phone calls from annoying cats?" a voice called from my doorway.

I jumped and spun around.

It was Alfreeda.

Ha! Who is she *to call someone else annoying?* I thought. *She doesn't ring the doorbell. Ever! And now she comes upstairs, totally uninvited, to my room! Where did she learn manners? From a litter of puppies?*

"Who *was* that super-annoying cat?" she asked. "It sure is a big crybaby! I hope it's not one of your hotel guests. That crying would drive you all crazy. Good thing most *dogs* aren't crybabies."

Before I knew what I was doing, I sprang off my bed. My face felt super hot.

"Don't you call that cat a crybaby!" I shouted. "Maybe cats cry sometimes.

Big deal! So what? What about *dogs*? Lots of them whine and bark and howl so loudly they give people headaches!"

Every hair on my head stood on end. My fingers curled into tight fists.

I was all set for a full-on catfight! No one makes fun of my Bootsie!

CHAPTER 4

Furry face-off!

I'd never shouted at anyone in my life. I didn't even know I was *able* to shout!

"Whoa," Alfreeda said. She held her hands in the air. "I came over to see if you wanted to have a sleepover tonight. But I can see someone's feeling catty. I better leave."

"Yes, you better leave!" I snapped. "And by the way, that was *my* cat you just called a crybaby. She's my best friend in the whole world. *Nobody* calls Bootsie mean names. Got it? Goodbye!"

"Oh. Okay. Sorry," Alfreeda said, backing into the corridor. Seconds later, I heard the kitchen door shut behind her.

I peeked down the corridor. Grandpa Tom's door was still closed. I couldn't believe he'd slept through that shouting match. But he always took his hearing aids out at night.

Now I headed past his door and downstairs to Tabby Towers. I'd clean litter boxes and kitty apartments until Bootsie arrived. The busier I was, the faster time would fly.

* * *

At last, in the middle of the morning, Pam and Bootsie arrived.

Grandma Kit and I were still busy in the hotel when the doorbell rang. We made sure the guests' apartment doors were shut tightly.

We never leave guests outside of their apartment if we're not there to watch them.

I ran to the front door and threw it open. Pam grinned and hugged me. She handed me Bootsie's carrier.

Grandma Kit headed to the car with Pam to gather Bootsie's things.

"Hi, Bootsie!" I said through the little door on the carrier. "My sweet girl! I can't believe you're here!"

She saw me and started to cry – quick, quiet, sad *meows*, over and over.

I threw open the carrier door, grabbed her and hugged her tightly. I buried my face in her fur. She smelled like soap.

She rolled over in my arms and lay there like a baby. I rocked her. She began to purr.

"*Now* we're happy," I said. "Come on, let's show everyone how much you'll love Tabby Towers. Let's prove how great you can get along with the other cats. All right?"

I carried her to the kitchen door and peeked inside. Scruffy was sound asleep in his bed. His back faced us.

Good, I thought. *Scruffy won't see Bootsie.* I had a strong feeling he wouldn't be nice to her. I'd make sure their paths wouldn't cross.

I tiptoed past Scruffy's bed and quietly entered the cat hotel. Softly, I shut the door behind us.

Then I held Bootsie right side up. "Look at the wonderful playground you'll get to play in," I said. "See the cat trees and the scratching posts? See the big rugs hanging on the walls? You can climb right up them and jump to those high shelves. Or you can jump to that big rope.

You can walk across it, like a tightrope walker in the circus. You'll have so much fun here!"

Bootsie purred and rubbed her cheek against mine. My heart leaped like a kitten on a toy.

I carried her to the big window at the rear of the room. "See the barn? See the chicken coop? Look at those pretty rolling hills! And that meadow filled with pretty flowers! You can sit here for hours and watch the chickens and Cheesecake the cow. You'll see birds and mice and snakes. You'll never be bored!"

Bootsie purred again.

"I *knew* you'd love it!" I cried. "Let's go see your kitty apartment. There's a lot of room to play in there too. You'll be so cozy and happy!"

I headed towards the row of apartments. I turned sideways so Bootsie wouldn't see the other guests – and for a very good reason.

I knew it's always important to introduce cats slowly. They never forget a *bad* first meeting.

I sidestepped towards Bootsie's apartment in the far corner. I hugged her tightly to my chest. She couldn't see the other cats. But she must've heard or smelled them.

It all happened so quickly I couldn't stop her. She climbed up my arm, her body stiffened and her back bowed. With a low, angry growl, she jumped onto my shoulder and sprang at Child's apartment.

I spun around. Everything happened in a split second. Bootsie's claws grabbed Child's screen door. Bootsie hung from the screen and hissed at Child.

Child backed into a corner of his apartment and hissed back.

Then Bootsie spat at Child. Child spat back!

The fur on both of the long-haired cats seemed to double in size. It was a furry face-off! I'd never seen anything like it!

"Bootsie!" I cried. "What are you doing? Calm down! *Calm down*!"

CHAPTER 5

Boots become gloves

Bootsie did *not* calm down.

She kept hanging on Child's screen door and hissing at him. And Child kept hissing right back at Bootsie.

I couldn't believe my sweet, gentle Bootsie was acting like this. I didn't even know she had meanness in her!

One thing I *did* know: I wasn't supposed to touch an angry cat. Ever. I could get bitten or clawed very badly.

But I wasn't thinking straight at that moment. I grabbed Bootsie and pulled her off Child's apartment door. I rushed her to the big window and faced the farmyard.

"Shhh," I whispered. "It's okay. It's okay. Just look outside at the nice chickens."

Bootsie shook all over. Her heart pounded.

I was *so* glad that her claws hadn't cut me when I'd grabbed her. "Of course you'd never hurt me, would you?" I whispered in her ear and rocked her. "You *are* my gentle girl, aren't you? You forgot that for a minute, right?"

I kept rocking her. Soon she stopped shaking. Her heartbeat slowed.

Now she lay upside-down in my arms, cradled like a doll. But she didn't purr. She looked across the room at the kitty apartments. Her tail hung down and started to wag.

Uh-oh, I thought. I grew worried again. Here's why: In the dog world, wagging tails mean happiness or excitement. In the cat world, a low-hanging, wagging tail means the cat is upset.

"It's okay," I whispered, rocking her more. "Everything is going to be fine. You'll make friends here. Soon you'll really love it."

The moment I said that, Bootsie looked straight at me. Her front leg swung back then swung forward, full force. Her paw hit me, right across my face!

My glasses flew across the room, hit the wall and landed on the floor.

"Bootsie!" I cried, dropping her onto Grandpa Tom's rocking chair.

Bootsie had never raised a paw at anyone in her life! Certainly not *me*!

I picked up my glasses and put them back on. One side sat higher than the other.

"Bootsie!" I cried again. "What's wrong with you? You bent my glasses! My new glasses. They cost a lot of money! How could you hit me? That was a very bad thing to do."

Bootsie looked away. She licked her front paw, the one that had struck me.

Suddenly her paws didn't look like boots anymore. They looked like boxing gloves. And Bootsie could certainly box!

My nose hurt. For the second time that morning, I felt like crying.

Then I remembered something I'd read about cats: If they can't fight a cat they're angry with, they'll fight the closest living thing. It's called sideways anger. Bootsie had boxed sideways – at *me*.

I sighed. "I understand, Bootsie. I really do," I said. "But you have to calm down and be nice. Then you and I can be together for the whole summer. Okay?"

I pet her head, and she purred.

"Good," I said, picking her up. "Come on. Let's go to the kitchen. I'll give you some raw eggs, straight from the chickens. And cream!

Straight from Cheesecake the cow! Would you like that? Huh? I bet those tasty treats will make you totally love it here."

I carried Bootsie into the kitchen. Pam and Grandma Kit sat at the table, sipping tea. They looked at us and smiled.

"So, how does Bootsie like her apartment and the other cats?" Grandma Kit asked.

"Um . . . ," I said, chewing my lip. I really didn't want to lie to Grandma Kit. I couldn't say everything was fine when my nose still hurt. My feelings still hurt too.

But I couldn't tell the truth either. If I did, Pam would take Bootsie straight back to the city. I couldn't let that happen.

Just then, Bootsie's body stiffened in my arms. She looked over my shoulder, in the direction of Scruffy's bed.

Oh no, I thought. I turned around slowly.

Scruffy was awake. And he was staring right at Bootsie.

She was staring at him too.

Their tails hung low and began to wag. Their backs bowed. Their fur stood on end.

Bootsie hissed and spat at Scruffy.

Scruffy hissed and spat at Bootsie.

Then my gentle, sweet cat sprang out of my arms and shot straight at Scruffy.

"Bootsie, NO!" I cried.

CHAPTER 6
Cat-paw cuff

The two angry cats went nose-to-nose. They kept hissing and spitting at each other.

Pam and Grandma Kit gasped. They jumped off their chairs.

I tried to grab Bootsie.

"No, Tabitha!" Grandma Kit warned. "Never come between two fighting cats!"

She grabbed a newspaper off the table and folded it in half. She dashed over and held the newspaper between the two spitting cats.

“This should break up the fight,” she said.

But Bootsie reached around the newspaper and *boxed* Scruffy right on the mouth!

Scruffy meowed and dove under the oven.

"Bootsie!" I cried, snatching her up.

"My, my, my!" Pam cried. "Sweet Bootsie cuffed another cat! Right on the kisser!"

I started to back out of the room. Pam shook her head sadly at me.

Grandma Kit sighed. "That's it," she said. "Tabitha, you need to say goodbye to Bootsie. She simply can't stay here. It wouldn't be healthy for her or the other cats."

No! I thought and raced out of the kitchen.

I hurried through the main floor and up the stairs. With every step, I felt more hope drain away.

I hurried to my room and shut the door. Bootsie leaped out of my arms and landed on my dresser. Her tail began to wag.

"Well, I'm upset too, Bootsie!" I groaned. "I don't want to be away from you all summer.

Even though you're not acting anything like my nice cat. *What* are we going to do?"

Someone knocked on my door.

Oh no, I thought. *It's Pam, coming to take Bootsie away!*

"Not yet!" I cried. "I haven't even had a chance to say goodbye!"

My door flew open. It was Alfreeda.

"Goodbye?" she laughed. "We haven't said hello yet!"

Without warning, the hair rose on top of my head and at the back of my neck.

"Would you *please* go away?" I hissed. "This is *my* room, *my* space. Can't you see that I need to be *alone* right now?"

CHAPTER 7

Leave me alone!

What was happening to me? Those were fighting words, and they shocked me the second they flew out of my mouth. I'd *never* said anything mean, to anyone!

But I couldn't stand it anymore. Alfreeda was like an annoying puppy that wouldn't leave me alone.

And I *really* needed to be alone just then. I had to think hard. I had to come up with a good plan quickly – a way to keep Bootsie at the farm, with me, all summer.

The problem was, Alfreeda wasn't moving. I narrowed my eyes and stared at her.

She stared back.

I refused to blink.

Alfreeda did too.

My eyes stung. A tear rolled down my cheek. Still, I didn't blink.

Neither did Alfreeda.

Pam called up the stairs, "Tabby? Tabby, are you up there?"

Alfreeda and I blinked at exactly the same time. I put a finger to my lips to tell her to be quiet. She nodded.

I didn't answer Pam. Bootsie jumped off the dresser and rubbed against my leg. She started to purr, and I picked her up.

"Tabby?" Pam called again. "Are you and Bootsie upstairs? Come on down. I've taken her things to the car. I'm sorry, but she and I need to leave now."

I put my finger to my lips again. Alfreeda nodded again. Bootsie stopped purring.

Pam's flip-flops slapped back to the kitchen. "I don't know. Maybe they went outside," she said to Grandma Kit. "Let's take a look."

The back door opened and shut.

"This way," I whispered to Alfreeda.

I tiptoed to the end of the corridor and up the attic stairs. Alfreeda followed. We went into the attic, and I shut the door behind us.

"What's going on?" Alfreeda asked quietly.

I sighed and told her the whole story. It took about a minute, start to finish.

"So," I finished, "when Pam and Grandma Kit find us up here, I'll have to kiss Bootsie goodbye. Pam might bring her for visits during July and August. But the visits won't be often enough. Bootsie is my *pet*! My *best* friend! Two weeks away from her has been bad enough."

"Wow," Alfreeda said. "That's really sad. No wonder you've acted so catty this morning. Put her down."

"Huh?" I said.

"Put Bootsie down," Alfreeda said. "Help me push this desk in front of the door. Pam and your grandma will never be able to get in."

"Okay!" I set Bootsie on the floor, and Alfreeda and I got busy.

We piled a few boxes on top of the desk. We pushed a heavy dresser and two old chairs against it too.

Tabby Towers
Hound Hotel

"They'll never be able to open the door," Alfreeda said.

"No, they really won't," I agreed. "Thanks."

"You're welcome."

Alfreeda and I sat in the chairs and waited for the battle to begin. Our backs faced the door. We had a wide view of the huge attic.

We heard Pam and Grandma Kit calling in the farmyard, "Tabby! Tabitha!"

We watched Bootsie tiptoe around every part of the room.

First, she batted balls of wool out of a small basket. Then, she scratched her claws on an old rug. Next, she dug into a large basket filled with winter hats and gloves.

"You know," Alfreeda said quietly, "no girls my age live anywhere near me. Not one.

That's why I was *so* excited when I heard you'd be staying at your grandparents' place all summer. My brother, Alfie? He drives me *crazy*. I really can't believe a girl my age is right next door now. I had hoped I could hang out over here a lot. To get away from Alfie. And, you know, to make a new friend."

I sighed. "I'm sorry I said those mean things."

"And I'm sorry I called Bootsie a crybaby," Alfreeda said.

"That's okay," I said. "She *was* crying a lot."

"Of course she was crying," Alfreeda said. "She missed you."

Alfreeda smiled at me. I smiled back.

We watched Bootsie dive into a deep box filled with rag dolls and doll clothes. When the silly cat came back out, she had a doll hat on her head. Alfreeda and I laughed.

"She's having fun up here," Alfreeda said.

"She is!" I agreed.

Tall shelves lined the walls. The shelves were filled with books, straw hats and empty vases. Several ladders leaned against the shelves.

Bootsie climbed one of the ladders. She moved across a top shelf, then leaped to a wooden beam near the roof.

With her usual excellent balance, she crept across the beam to the far wall. She sat on the beam and peered out a small window.

Right outside the window, a dove sat in a nest. Bootsie peered at the bird as if she were watching the best film ever made.

Just then, footsteps pounded on the attic stairs. The door handle turned. Of course, the door didn't open. Not with all that weight piled in front of it.

Someone knocked on the door.

"Tabby?" Pam said in her firm nanny voice. "Open up."

"No more foolishness, Tabitha," Grandma Kit said. "Bootsie needs to go back to the city with Pam. And I need to get back to work in the hotel. Come out – now."

CHAPTER 8

The purr-fect plan

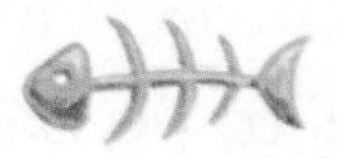

Seconds passed. I didn't say anything to Pam or Grandma Kit.

I hated being rude to them. My heart wouldn't stop pounding.

I couldn't take my eyes off Bootsie. And she couldn't take her eyes off the dove outside the window. It seemed that Bootsie could sit there forever, happily watching that songbird.

"*This* could be Bootsie's territory!" I said, snapping my fingers. "Scruffy never comes up here. This isn't part of his territory at all!"

"Cool!" Alfreeda nodded excitedly.

I pointed across the room.

"Those high shelves?" I said. "They could be cleared off. Bootsie would have a blast climbing to all the high places. She'd *love* the piles of old clothes and blankets and rag dolls. She could sleep in these cozy old chairs. She could spend hours looking out that little window at the farmyard below."

"Yeah," Alfreeda said. "And we could find more scratching posts for her. And bring in lots of cat toys. She'd love it up here!"

"And she wouldn't have to share the space with any other cats," I said.

"I'll help you turn this attic into a super-fun kitty playground," Alfreeda offered.

"Thanks," I said with a grin. "That would be great. Just great!"

⁂

Ten minutes later, we'd pushed the furniture away, opened the door and shared the plan.

Grandma Kit loved the idea. Pam thought it was a good one too.

The four of us carried Bootsie's things to the attic, then Pam hugged me goodbye.

"Bye to you, Bootsie!" Pam called.

But Bootsie didn't take her eyes off that dove, not for a second.

⁂

Alfreeda and I spent all afternoon turning the attic into a purr-fect kitty playground.

First, we brought in a big old log with branches. We put one end in a large pot and turned it into a cat tree.

Next, we folded a lot of colourful paper birds and hung them in the tree. Bootsie would have a blast boxing those.

Then we hung a rug on the wall for Bootsie to climb. We also cleared off high shelves and put cozy kitty beds on the highest spots.

"I have a lot of art and craft stuff at my house," Alfreeda said. "I could bring some over. We could make cat toys and cat games."

"Sure!" I said.

Alfreeda and I worked into the evening. Grandpa Tom brought dinner to the attic for us. Bootsie came off the beam to eat her dinner too. When she finished, I gave her a long hug. I had a feeling she had hung up her boxing gloves for good.

Alfreeda and I were still busy making cat toys near bedtime.

Grandpa Tom brought us a late-night popcorn snack. "Why don't you two sleep up here tonight?" he said. "Alfreeda, I'll check with your mum and make sure it's okay. I'm sure it will be. You girls can keep Bootsie company during her first night on the farm. There are plenty of blankets for you two."

"Great idea! Thanks, Grandpa," I said.

Alfreeda and I got busy making cozy beds for ourselves. Then I said good night to Bootsie.

But she was back on the beam, back in "her" spot, watching the sleeping dove and the gleaming stars.

Is a Himalayan cat the cat for you?

Hello, it's me, Tabitha!

I'm sure you'd LOVE your own beautiful Himalayan cat now, right? Of course you would! They make wonderful pets for families with children.

Here's why: Himalayan cats are a cross between Persian and Siamese cats. (They have the long hair of a Persian and the colouring of a Siamese.) They are as gentle as a Persian and as curious as a Siamese. Most Himalayan cats are usually calm, kind and friendly.

Now you REALLY want a Himalayan cat, correct? Well, before you buy or adopt one, there are some important things you should know:

Himalayan cats must be groomed every day. All of their hair must be combed or brushed daily, all over their body. If it isn't, the hair will tangle and cause discomfort. Also, because cats groom themselves by licking their fur, uncombed Himalayan cats could get large balls of hair in their stomach. That could be deadly for the cat.

Himalayan cats sometimes have health problems. They may have problems with their joints, skin, eyes or kidneys. They may also have breathing problems. It's important that Himalayan cat owners plan regular checkups with a vet.

Himalayan cats are less active than many other types of cats. They can become overweight quite easily. They must not be overfed.

All right, cat lovers! That's all for now . . . until the next adventure at Tabby Towers!

Meowingly yours,

Tabitha Catarina Felinus (Tabby Cat, for short)

Glossary

annoying making someone feel angry or impatient

groom to brush and clean an animal

instinct behaviour that is natural rather than learned

litter box tray filled with bits of wood, paper or clay in which cats go to the bathroom

nocturnal active at night and resting during the day

predator animal that hunts other animals for food

prey animal hunted by another animal for food

territorial strongly guarding one's space

territory area of land that an animal claims as its own to live in

vet doctor who cares for animals

Talk about it

1. On page 25, Grandma Kit tells her granddaughter, "You're learning to think like a cat, Tabby Cat." Describe how Tabby also *looks* and *acts* like a cat. Share examples from the text and illustrations to support your answer.

2. Bootsie makes Tabby the target of her sideways anger when she knocks off the girl's glasses. Explain what the term "sideways anger" means. Then describe a time when you released some sideways anger like Bootsie did. Who was your target? And at whom (or what) were you *really* angry?

Write about it

1. If Bootsie could talk, how do you think she would describe the adventure she had at Tabby Towers? Write a paragraph from Bootsie's point of view.

2. Write a letter to your parents that explains why you think a Himalayan would, or would not, be a good cat for your family.

3. Write a one-page essay on Himalayan cats. Be sure to use at least three sources.

About the author

Shelley Swanson Sateren has been a freelance writer for thirty years and has written more than forty books for children, both fiction and non-fiction. As well as writing, Shelley has worked as a children's book editor and in a children's bookshop. She is also a primary school teacher and has enjoyed employment in several schools. Shelley lives in Minnesota, USA, with her husband and has two grown-up sons.

About the illustrator

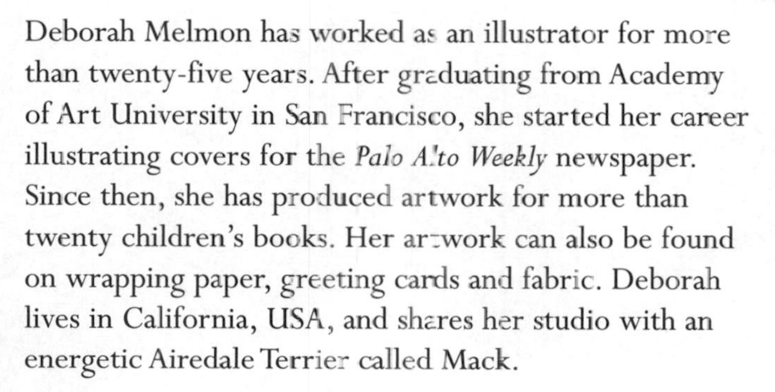

Deborah Melmon has worked as an illustrator for more than twenty-five years. After graduating from Academy of Art University in San Francisco, she started her career illustrating covers for the *Palo Alto Weekly* newspaper. Since then, she has produced artwork for more than twenty children's books. Her artwork can also be found on wrapping paper, greeting cards and fabric. Deborah lives in California, USA, and shares her studio with an energetic Airedale Terrier called Mack.

VISIT

TABBY TOWERS

AGAIN WITH

THESE AWESOME

ADVENTURES!

ADVENTURES at
TABBY TOWERS
Leaping Lizzie
Queen Lizzie's Pizza Palace
Written by
Sateren
Illustrated by
Deborah Melmon
ADVENTURES at
TABBY TOWERS
Boxing Bootsie
Written by
Shelley Swanson Sateren
Illustrated by
Deborah Melmon
ADVENTURES at
TABBY TOWERS
Disappearing Darcy
Written by
Shelley Swanson Sateren
Illustrated by
Deborah Melmon
ADVENTURES at
TABBY TOWERS
Fishing Frankie
Written by
Shelley Swanson Sateren
Illustrated by
Deborah Melmon

(WE PROMISED ALFREEDA
WE'D INCLUDE THE
HOUND HOTEL GUESTS
AND THEIR SUPER-FUN
STORIES HERE TOO!)
www.raintree.co.uk
ADVENTURES AT HOUND HOTEL
Cool Crosby
ADVENTURES AT HOUND HOTEL
Drooling Dudley
ADVENTURES AT HOUND HOTEL
Fearless Freddie
ADVENTURES AT HOUND HOTEL
Growling Gracie
ADVENTURES AT HOUND HOTEL
Homesick Herbie
ADVENTURES AT HOUND HOTEL
Mighty Murphy
ADVENTURES AT HOUND HOTEL
Mudball Molly
ADVENTURES AT HOUND HOTEL
Stinky Stanley